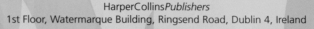

DEAN

First published in Great Britain 2016 by Farshore
This edition published in Great Britain 2021 by Dean
An imprint of HarperCollins*Publishers*
1 London Bridge Street, London SE1 9GF
www.farshore.co.uk

HarperCollins*Publishers*
1st Floor, Watermarque Building, Ringsend Road, Dublin 4, Ireland

HiT entertainmen

PB ISBN 978 0 0084 9472 8
5 book set ISBN 978 0 0085 0015 3
10 book set ISBN 978 0 0084 9794 1
Printed in Great Britain
001

Trevor has volunteered to take everyone to the Christmas Festival in Newtown.

"Hurry up, Norman!" calls Dilys. "It's starting to **snow!"**

The snow falls **faster** and **faster**. Soon, Trevor can't see out of his window!

SCREECH! The bus skids off the icy road, and onto a frozen lake. "I'd better call for help," says Trevor.

Who would you call for help?

Charlie

Fireman Sam

Radar

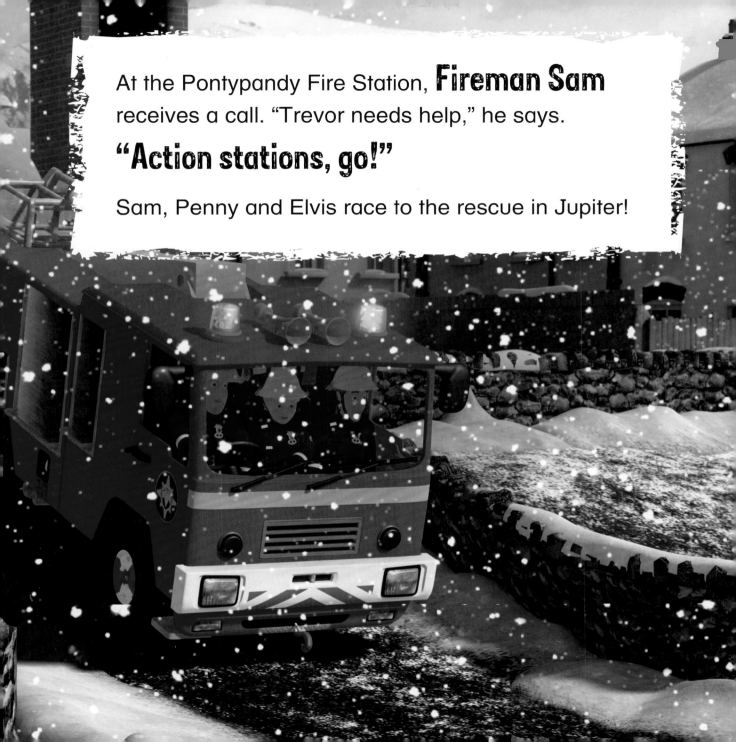

At the Pontypandy Fire Station, **Fireman Sam** receives a call. "Trevor needs help," he says.

"Action stations, go!"

Sam, Penny and Elvis race to the rescue in Jupiter!

CRACK! The ice underneath the bus is starting to break!

"Everyone stand back," says Sam. "We need to rescue the bus."

What would you use to rescue the bus?

tow line

axe

fire hose

Sam hooks up the tow line. Jupiter pulls the bus back to safety.

"Steady!" calls Penny. "The ice is slippery."

The bus is saved! But it's still snowing, and Sarah is starting to shiver.

"I'm so c-c-cold!" she says.

"You need to warm up," says Sam.

What would you give Sarah to warm up?

life jacket

sunglasses

warm drink and blanket

Penny gives Sarah a **warm blanket** and a cup of hot chocolate. Soon Sarah feels much better!

As soon as the snow clears, Trevor says, "Now we can all go to the **Christmas Festival!**"

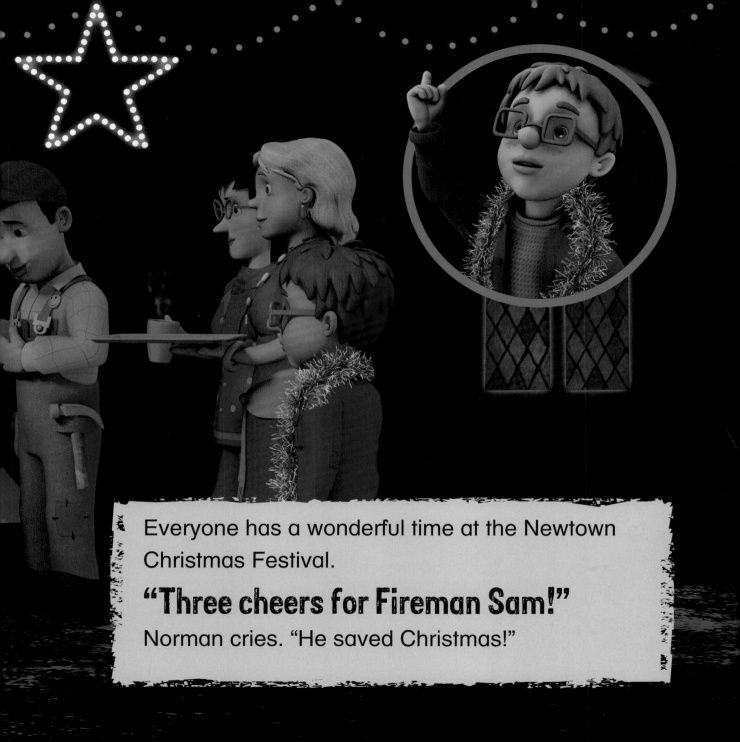

Everyone has a wonderful time at the Newtown Christmas Festival.

"Three cheers for Fireman Sam!"

Norman cries. "He saved Christmas!"

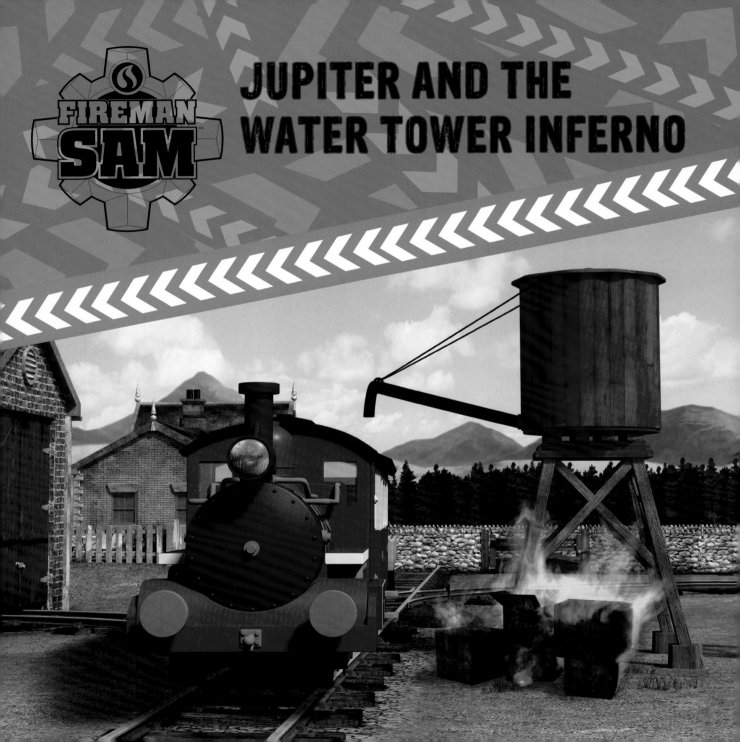

JUPITER AND THE
WATER TOWER INFERNO

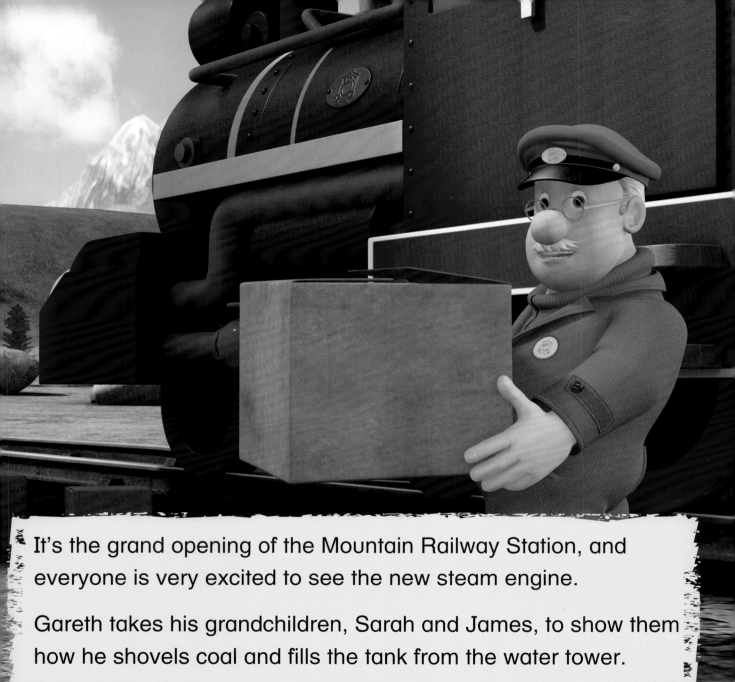

It's the grand opening of the Mountain Railway Station, and everyone is very excited to see the new steam engine.

Gareth takes his grandchildren, Sarah and James, to show them how he shovels coal and fills the tank from the water tower.

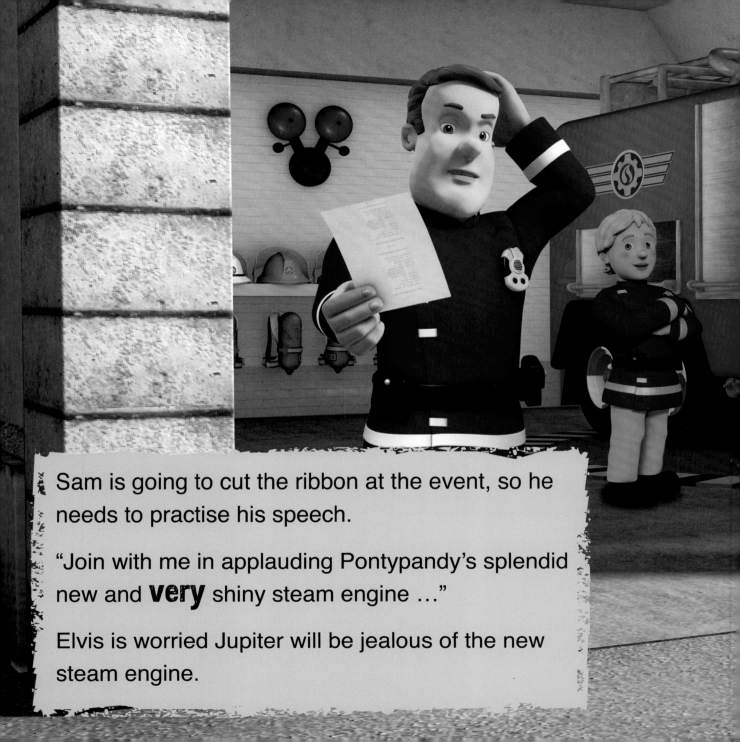

Sam is going to cut the ribbon at the event, so he needs to practise his speech.

"Join with me in applauding Pontypandy's splendid new and **very** shiny steam engine …"

Elvis is worried Jupiter will be jealous of the new steam engine.

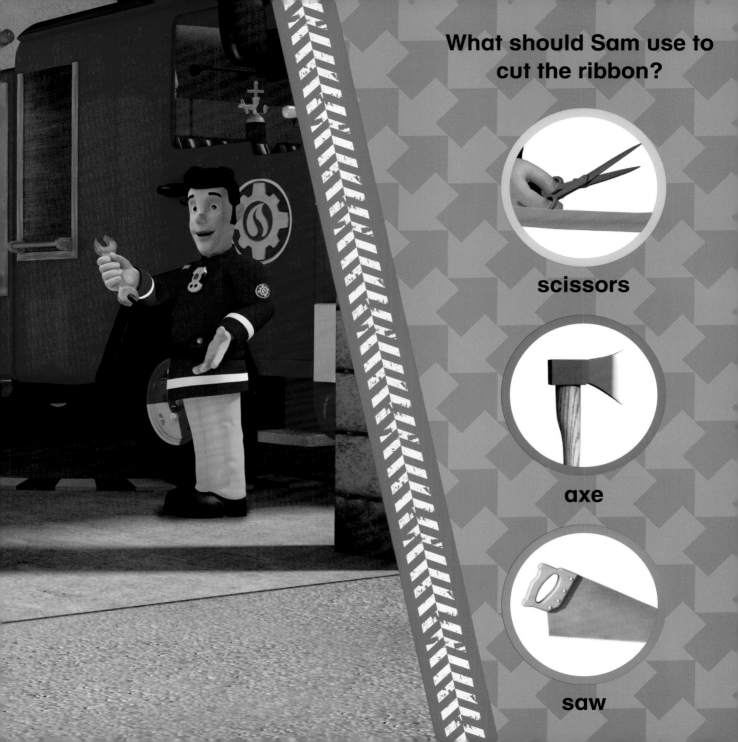

What should Sam use to cut the ribbon?

scissors

axe

saw

Gareth shovels coal into the train's furnace while James and Sarah decorate the railway station for the big event.

James takes a **tumble** and ends up in trouble. Gareth quickly runs to the rescue, but he knocks a piece of **hot coal** into a box of bunting.

Soon the grand opening begins and the passengers arrive excited to have a ride in the Pontypandy Flyer.

"There's a fire!" they shout, when they discover the box has caught fire and has spread to the water tower.

Who should the crowd call for help?

Fireman Sam

Norman

Radar

Sam and Elvis arrive at the scene with Jupiter. Penny follows in Venus. Sam quickly gets to work.

"Stay back, everyone," he says. "The tower is very heavy and it could **collapse** at any moment."

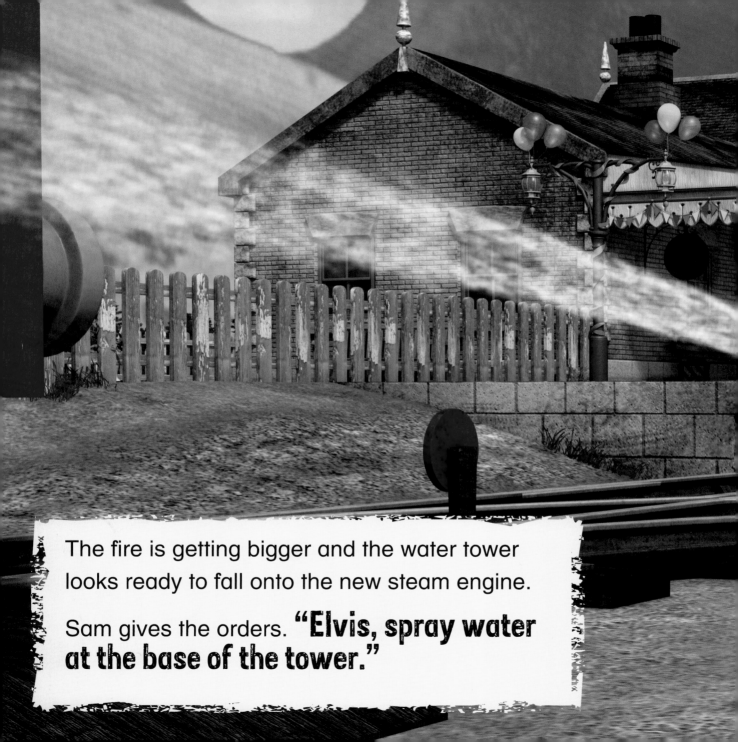

The fire is getting bigger and the water tower looks ready to fall onto the new steam engine.

Sam gives the orders. **"Elvis, spray water at the base of the tower."**

"Penny, drive Venus up to the front of the train."

Sam rushes up and ties a big metal tow rope to the front of the engine.

Slowly **Venus** begins to move backwards, pulling the train clear of the tower just as it **collapses!**

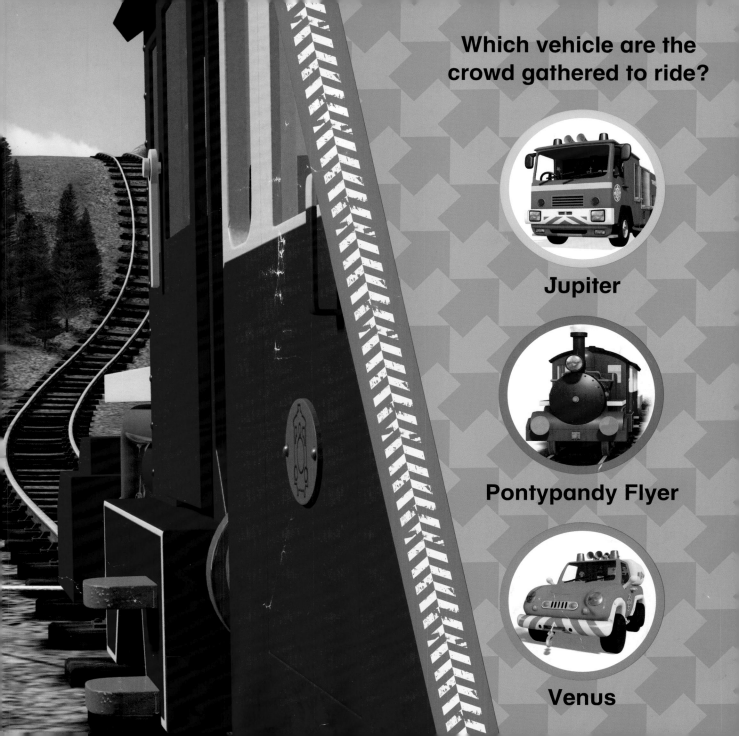

Which vehicle are the crowd gathered to ride?

Jupiter

Pontypandy Flyer

Venus

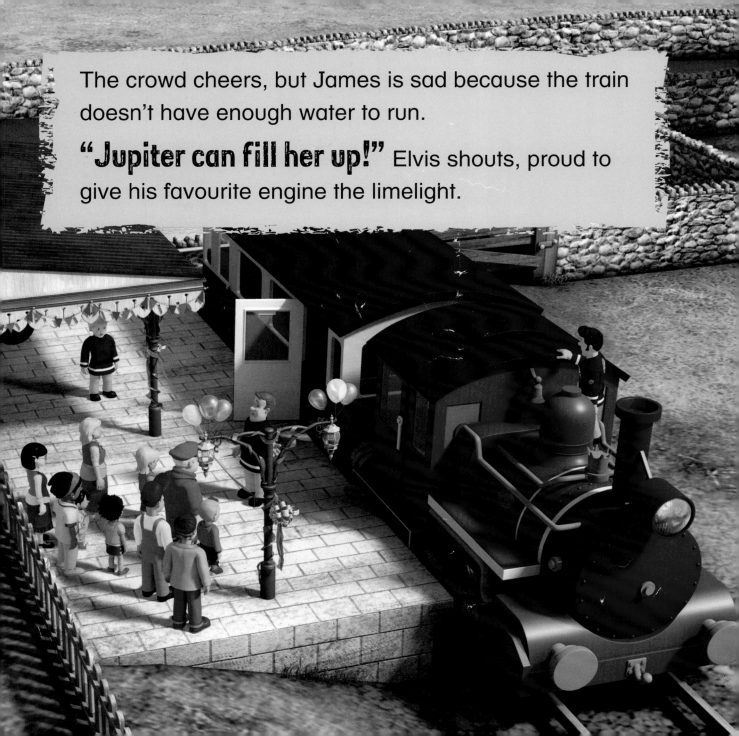

The crowd cheers, but James is sad because the train doesn't have enough water to run.

"Jupiter can fill her up!" Elvis shouts, proud to give his favourite engine the limelight.